To all my Eleanors:
Mother, Grandmother,
Goddaughter and friends,
with love - T.K.

For my three lovely boys,
Stanley, Atticus and Albert - D.T.

SIMON AND SCHUSTER
First published in Great Britain in 2013
by Simon and Schuster UK Ltd
1st Floor, 222 Gray's Inn Road, London, WC1X 8HB
A CBS Company

A CIP catalogue record for this book is available from the
British Library upon request

978-0-85707-840-7 (HB)
978-0-85707-841-4 (PB)
978-1-4711-1627-8 (eBook)
Printed in China
10 9 8 7 6 5 4 3 2 1

Eleanor's Eyebrows

TIMOTHY KNAPMAN

Eleanor's Eyebrows

Illustrated by
DAVID TAZZYMAN

SIMON AND SCHUSTER
London   New York   Sydney   Toronto   New Delhi

Eleanor knew EXACTLY what all
the different bits of her face were for...

Her eyes were
    for crossing.

Her ears were
for waggling.

Her nose was
    for picking.

And her tongue was
for sticking
    out at people.

BUT....

"What on earth is the point of eyebrows?" said Eleanor one day. "They're just two silly, scruffy, hairy, little bits of fluff!"

Now, Eleanor's eyebrows wouldn't
stay where they weren't wanted.

So that night, while Eleanor slept,
they slid off her face and ventured out
into the Big Wide World to find someone
who would love them for what they were.

And that's when they saw a notice.

ARE YOU LONG, THIN AND HAIRY?

Want to be MORE than just a silly, scruffy, hairy, little bit of fluff?

We can make you BEAUTIFUL!

Come to the BUTTERFLY HOUSE at the ZOO!

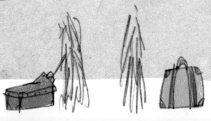

So the eyebrows made straight for the zoo, and in no time they were tucked up in the Butterfly House.

It was full of caterpillars who were fluffy and hairy too!

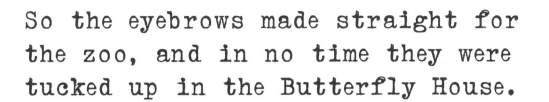

BUT...

...the eyebrows didn't like the taste of leaves. And no matter how hard they worked at it, they just couldn't make cocoons.

So the eyebrows went looking for another home.

They tried being a twirling moustache for a **marvellous magician.**

BUT...

...they tried being woolly handwarmers for beautiful lady beetles who didn't want to catch cold.

And false legs for a very large ant who liked pretending to be a spider and...

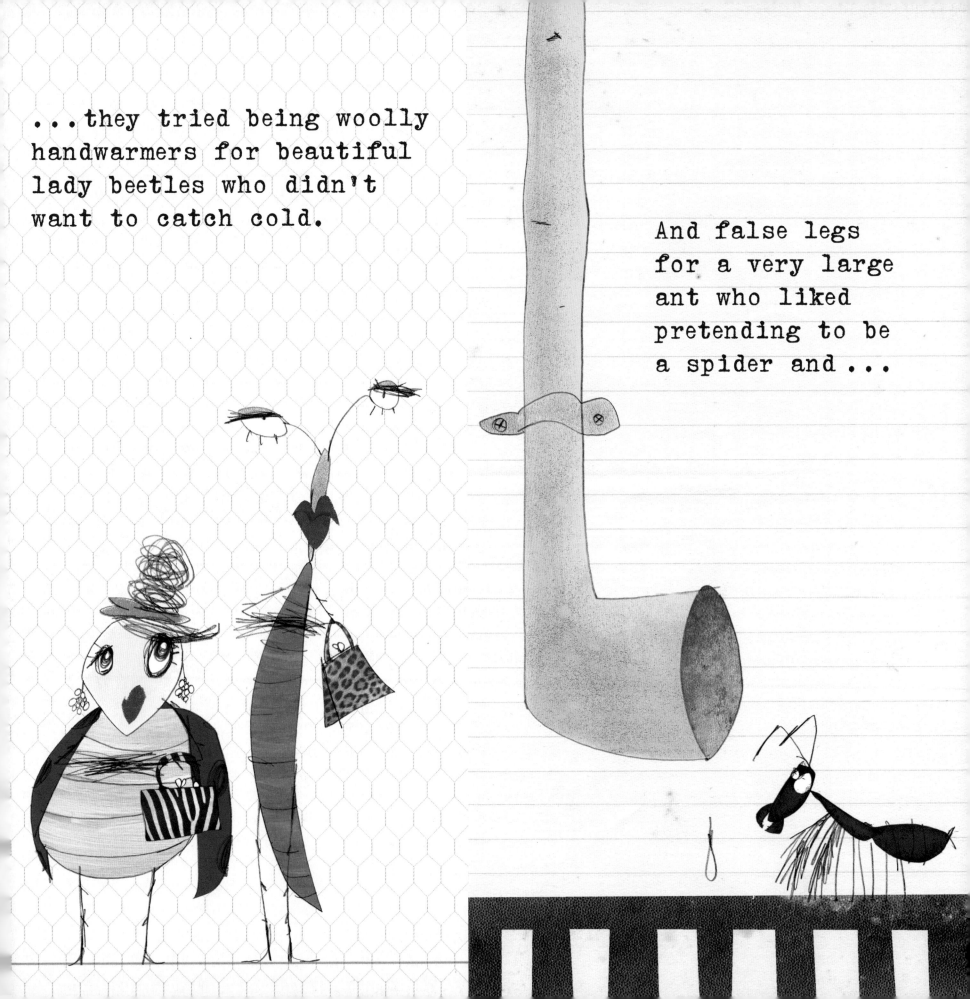

...tyres on a stick insect's motorbike.

Eleanor, meanwhile, had been merrily
getting on with life. She hadn't missed
her eyebrows one little bit until, one day,
her Granny came to visit.

The old lady took one look at the empty
space above Eleanor's eyes ...

... and screamed and ran a mile.

"Is THAT all it is?" said Eleanor, looking in the mirror.

"Well, I can easily draw some **EYEBROWS** on!"

But Eleanor wasn't very good at drawing.

No matter how many times she tried.

So instead she combed her hair forward.

But it just got in her eyes and made her **bump** into things.

Then she tried balancing her pet mice on her face.

But they just bit her and fell off.

Suddenly, wherever Eleanor went,
all she noticed were eyebrows.

Squiggly eyebrows and fat eyebrows.

Sensible eyebrows and mad eyebrows.
Eyebrows with shiny silver rings through them.
Eyebrows like flashes of lightning.

Eyebrows that met in the middle
and eyebrows that were so far apart
they could almost be ear hair.

She had never realised how wild and wonderful
eyebrows were, and how much she missed her own.

"I'm so miserable without my lovely eyebrows," said Eleanor. "I wish I could get them back! But how?"

And then she had a brilliant idea.

Are you long,
thin and hai

Meanwhile, out in the Big Wide World, Eleanor's eyebrows had got a job as an exclamation mark on a very angry sign.

But it rained and they got washed off.

Suddenly, the eyebrows felt cold and wet
and a long, long way from home.
And that's when they saw a notice.

When Eleanor woke up the next morning,
the space above her eyes felt itchy.

"What's gone wrong now?" she wondered sadly.
So she looked at her face in the mirror.

And there, right above her eyes were
HER EYEBROWS!

And now Eleanor
knew **EXACTLY** what
they were for . . .

...making her

HAPPY!